KEEPUNUMUK

WEEÂCHUMUN'S THANKSGIVING STORY

Danielle Greendeer,
Anthony Perry,
and Alexis Bunten

Illustrated by
Garry Meeches Sr.

Charlesbridge

We dedicate *Keepunumuk* to our children, who are our ancestors' dreams come true—D. G., A. P., and A. B.

I'd like to dedicate *Keepunumuk* to our future generations to remember the stories of the past to carry forward to their children and grandchildren—G. M.

Thank you to the Wôpanâak Language Reclamation Project for their dedication to preserving our sacred language.

Published by Charlesbridge
9 Galen Street, Watertown, MA 02472
(617) 926-0329 • www.charlesbridge.com

Illustrations done in acrylic
Hand lettering by Ellie Erhart
Text type set in Today by Veronika Elsner and Bold Riley by Simon Stratford
Color separations by Colourscan Print Co Pte Ltd, Singapore
Printed by 1010 Printing International Limited in Huizhou, Guangdong, China
Production supervision by Jennifer Most Delaney
Designed by Diane M. Earley

Library of Congress Cataloging-in-Publication Data
Names: Greendeer, Danielle, author. | Perry, Anthony (Children's author), author. | Bunten, Alexis C., author. | Meeches, Garry, illustrator.
Title: Keepunumuk: Weeâchumun's Thanksgiving story / Danielle Greendeer, Anthony Perry, and Alexis Bunten; illustrated by Garry Meeches Sr.
Description: Watertown, MA: Charlesbridge Publishing, [2021] | Audience: Ages 3–7. | Audience: Grades K–1. | Summary: Wampanoag children listen as their grandmother tells them the story about how Weeâchumun (the wise Corn) asked local Native Americans to show the newcomers how to grow food to yield a good harvest—Keepunumuk—in 1621.
Identifiers: LCCN 2020026147 (print) | LCCN 2020026148 (ebook) | ISBN 9781623542900 (hardcover) | ISBN 9781632899217 (ebook)
Subjects: CYAC: Thanksgiving Day—Fiction. | Wampanoag Indians—Fiction. | Indians of North America—Massachusetts—Fiction. | newcomers (New Plymouth Colony)—Fiction.
Classification: LCC PZ7.1.H5613 Ke 2021 (print) | LCC PZ7.1.H5613 (ebook) | DDC [E]—dc23
LC record available at https://lccn.loc.gov/2020026147
LC ebook record available at https://lccn.loc.gov/2020026148

Printed in China
(hc) 10 9 8 7 6 5 4 3

BEFORE YOU BEGIN

This is the tale of the harvest feast shared by the newcomers and the Wampanoag people in 1621. The newcomers arrived in what is now Plymouth, Massachusetts, and colonized the ancestral homeland of the Wampanoag tribes. At the time of this first Thanksgiving, many tribes lived in the same area. They are often known as "Indians" or "Native Americans." In this story we call them First Peoples because they were the first to live on this land. The Wampanoag people have taken care of their land and tended their gardens for at least 12,000 years. The Wampanoag people hunt, fish, and raise the Three Sisters: Corn, Beans, and Squash. Over time, First Peoples developed deep knowledge about the ways that many plants—often called "medicine"— help bodies and minds stay healthy.

IMPORTANT WORDS TO KNOW

In the past and still today, Wampanoag people speak a language called Wôpanâak. There are some Wôpanâak words and concepts in the story.

Keepunumuk (KEE-puh-nuh-muk): the time of harvest

nasamp (nah-somp): a traditional Wampanoag dish

N8hkumuhs (NOO-kuh-mus): Grandmother

Ousamequin (ooh-sah-MEE-quan): a leader of the Wampanoag tribes; also known as Massasoit (mass-uh-SOH-it)

succotash (SUC-COH-tash): soup made from corn, beans, and squash

Tisquantum (tih-SQUAN-tum): a Wampanoag man; also known as Squanto

Turtle Island: a name used by many First Peoples for North America, based on traditional stories

Wampanoag (womp-a-NAH-ahg): a First Peoples tribe; means "People of the First Light"

"I love your garden this time of year," said Maple.

"Me, too. What shall we pick for lunch?" N8hkumuhs asked.

"How about crab apples?" Maple suggested.

"No! Chokecherries!" Quill shouted.

"Those are both good medicine," N8hkumuhs said. "How about some weeâchumun, as well?"

"Yes!" Maple replied. "She is such a good big sister to Beans and Squash."

"The Three Sisters! They grow together," Quill added.

"You're right. They feed people all over Turtle Island," N8hkumuhs said. "And they have many stories to tell."

"Can you tell us a story?" Quill asked.

"How about the time Weeâchumun asked our Wampanoag ancestors to help the Pilgrims?" N8hkumuhs replied.

"The first Thanksgiving?" Maple asked.

"Some people call it that," N8hkumuhs said. "We call it Keepunumuk, the time of harvest. Here's what really happened."

One frosty fall morning, a long time ago, a large
boat with white sails approached the shore.
Seagull circled above the boat, squawking,
"New people are coming!
New people are coming!"

Hearing the news, Weeâchumun stretched her weary ears toward the sky. "Who are these new people?" she asked.

Two winters had passed since many of the
First Peoples who cared for Weeâchumun
passed on to the Spirit World. Those who
were not taken by sickness found new
homes to ease their heavy hearts and
rebuild their lives.

Weeâchumun feared this winter would be
her last and called upon Fox for help.

Fox looked up at Weeâchumun. "Should
we trust these newcomers?" he asked.

"Stay close and watch what they do,"
Weeâchumun told Fox.

Fall turned to winter.

Weeâchumun and the other plants fell asleep.

Fox watched the newcomers come ashore.

He watched as they made their way into the forest.

He watched them enter an abandoned wetu.

He watched them take a cooking pot and a basket
   of Weeâchumun's seeds.
"Don't take us away!" the seeds cried. "We are
   waiting for the First Peoples to come
   back in the spring to prepare our beds.
   We must grow first!"
But the newcomers could not hear the
   seeds. Their ears did not know
   the voices of the land.

Fox watched the newcomers build homes
on top of an empty village.
He watched as they searched for food, but
they could never find enough to eat.
Many of the newcomers lost mothers,
fathers, brothers, and sisters during the
long, cold winter.

The First Peoples watched as well. News traveled fast among nearby tribes that newcomers had arrived. Nobody was sure what to make of them. For many years, others had traveled across the sea to hunt, fish, and trade. Some were friendly, and some were not. These new people seemed different. They were here to stay.

Winter turned into spring.

The sun warmed the earth. The newcomers continued their search for food.

Weeâchumun awoke from her long slumber and thanked the Creator for another season. She and her sisters, Beans and Squash, pushed through the ground and reached toward the sky.

Fox returned to share what he had seen.

"The newcomers are hungry," Fox told the three sisters. "They took Weeâchumun's seeds, but they don't know how to help them grow."

Other animals came to hear what Fox had to say.

"We should help," Weeâchumun said.

"I agree," Beans said. "Our home is their home now."

"I think we should, too," said Squash. "People help us grow."

"We must help," Deer said. "We agreed to feed the people. In return they care for the home we share."

"I wouldn't," said Fox. "The newcomers don't
know our world."

"Sometimes new people can seem scary," Rabbit
said. "The Creator tells us to help all living
things. This is how the world works."

"Yes!" Duck and Turkey agreed.

"It's settled," said Weeâchumun. "We will
send the First Peoples to help
the newcomers."

Over the next few nights, Weeâchumun sent
dreams to the First Peoples with a message:

Bring me and my sisters to the newcomers.
They are hungry and need help.

The First Peoples listened.

Their leader, Ousamequin, visited the
newcomers. He could see that they
wanted peace.
Ousamequin introduced the newcomers
to Tisquantum.

Spring turned into summer.
Tisquantum showed the newcomers how to
   raise Weeâchumun and her sisters, Beans
   and Squash. He taught the newcomers how
   to feed fish and seaweed to Weeâchumun
   to help her grow.

Soon Weeâchumun's seeds pushed through the earth
and climbed toward the sky.
Beans wrapped around Weeâchumun's strong stalks.
Squash stretched her vines across the ground, keeping
Weeâchumun's bed cool and moist.

Summer turned to fall.

Weeâchumun brimmed with food. So did Beans
and Squash.

Weeâchumun smiled as the newcomers thanked
Tisquantum and the First Peoples for their help.

Keepunumuk, the time of harvest, had come.

The newcomers prepared a feast to celebrate the first year in their new home. They fired muskets in celebration. *Boom! Boom! Boom!* Ousamequin, warriors, and other First Peoples arrived. They feasted for three days.

That meal changed both our lives and theirs forever.
Many Americans call it a day of thanksgiving.
Many of our people call it a day of mourning.

"That's different from what we learn in school," said Maple. "It was Weeâchumun and the other beings of the land, sea, and sky who made the newcomers' first harvest possible?"

"That's right," N8hkumuhs said. "This is why we pray before we eat."

"Well, what did the newcomers and our ancestors eat, N8hkumuhs?" Quill asked.

"Many things! Succotash, duck, turkey, rabbit, deer, lobster, fish, pumpkins, cranberries, boiled bread, and nasamp," N8hkumuhs said.

"All this talk about food is making me hungry," Maple said. "Let's go make us some lunch, then." N8hkumuhs laughed. "And we'll enjoy every bite!" said Quill.

ABOUT THE WAMPANOAG TRIBES

The Mashpee Wampanoag people live in the Cape Cod area of Massachusetts and call themselves the "People of the First Light." There were sixty-nine Wampanoag tribes living in Southeastern Massachusetts at the time the newcomers arrived. These settlers included religious Separatists (later known as Pilgrims) and traders who were the first to colonize the Wampanoag homeland. Colonization is when a group of people take land by force from another group to permanently live there and control resources. Colonization has had a devastating effect on all First Peoples. Today, the state of Massachusetts is home to only two federally recognized tribes: the Mashpee Wampanoag Tribe and the Wampanoag Tribe of Gay Head (Aquinnah).

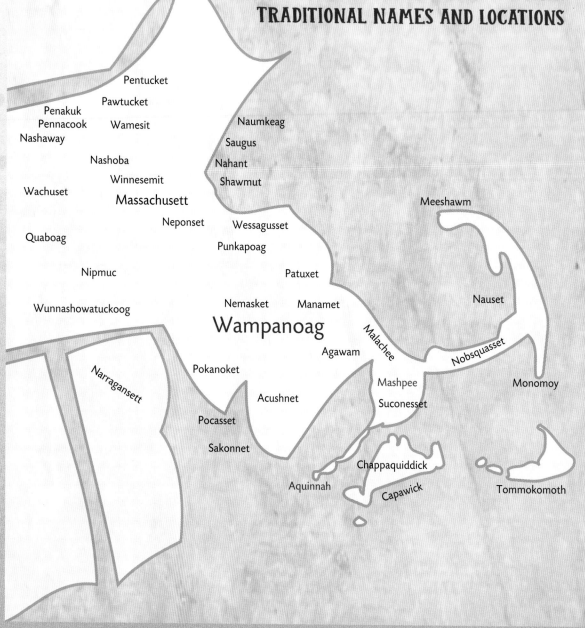

TRIBAL NATIONS: TRADITIONAL NAMES AND LOCATIONS

Pentucket
Pawtucket
Penakuk
Pennacook
Wamesit
Nashaway
Naumkeag
Saugus
Nahant
Nashoba
Shawmut
Winnesemit
Wachuset
Massachusett
Neponset
Wessagusset
Quaboag
Punkapoag
Nipmuc
Patuxet
Wunnashowatuckoog
Nemasket
Manamet
Wampanoag
Agawam
Malachee
Nauset
Nobsquasset
Pokanoket
Mashpee
Narragansett
Acushnet
Suconesset
Monomoy
Pocasset
Sakonnet
Chappaquiddick
Aquinnah
Capawick
Tommokomoth
Meeshawm

with permission from Aaron Carapella

THE WAMPANOAG STORYTELLING TRADITION

Storytelling is very important to the Wampanoag people. Elders tell stories to pass on knowledge about culture, tribal history, and traditions, such as how to plant the Three Sisters. We know only the English settlers' version of the "first Thanksgiving" from their written records. Sadly, the Wampanoag side of the story was lost after a majority of tribal members died from warfare and disease introduced by these newcomers. But fortunately, many Wampanoag stories have survived and are still told today. This book is a new story that shares the traditional Wampanoag understanding about the sacred relationship between Weeâchumun and human beings.

WAMPANOAG HARVEST FEASTS

In addition to a fall harvest feast that celebrates corn, the Wampanoag people come together for many harvest feasts throughout the year, including Strawberry Thanksgiving, Herring Day, and Quahog Day. Many New England tribes think of the Thanksgiving holiday as a "Day of Mourning," because the settlers brought disease and warfare that continue to take the lives of many Indigenous people today. Each year, they come together at Plymouth Rock in Massachusetts to remember their ancestors who have passed on to the Spirit World. Even today, the Wampanoag people—and many other First Peoples—fight for their rights as sovereign Nations to practice their traditions, make their own laws, and live on their homelands.

TRY A WAMPANOAG TRADITION OF GIVING THANKS

For the Wampanoag people, guardian spirits take the form of animals and plants, like Weeâchumun, to watch over human beings. The Wampanoag people honor guardian spirits as well as loved ones who have left this world. Before special meals they make a plate of food for the spirits to eat and place it outside. Try making a Spirit Plate at your next gathering in gratitude for plants, animals, and ancestors. Take a pinch of each food served at the meal and put the plate in a special place outside. When you make a Spirit Plate, think about people you love who have passed on. You can give thanks to plants and animals and make good wishes for others.

MAKE A WAMPANOAG RECIPE

Nasamp is a traditional Wampanoag dish made from cornmeal, nuts, berries, and fresh maple syrup, boiled in water until it thickens. Children should always get help from an adult before using the stove.

1 cup cornmeal
1 cup dried or fresh berries
¼ cup crushed walnuts, sunflower seeds, or other nuts
2 cups water
maple syrup to taste

Combine all ingredients except the maple syrup in a pot and boil for 5 minutes.

Turn down the heat and simmer, stirring frequently, for about 15 minutes or until all water is absorbed.

Spoon into bowls and drizzle maple syrup on top.

MEET MAPLE AND QUILL

The real Maple and Quill are Mashpee Wampanoag kids who live in Mashpee, Massachusetts. In this photo, Maple is four, Quill is two, and baby Tulsi is twelve months old. Maple likes to pick flowers with her mom. Quill likes to fish with his dad. They both love to spend time listening to their grandmother, Nokomis (noh-KOH-mus), tell them Wampanoag stories.